(Chapter 1)

Looking back over my years on this wild and crazy planet I've got to say. I have experienced so many wild and crazy incidents during my life. I was born a twin at birth. Shortly after my brother and I were to breath our first breaths of life we would lose him. Johnathan David Lilly my twin brother my new best friend if only for a few moments in time.

After the loss of him my life changed FOREVER. And in a very big way. I would experience so many out of this world moments. Seeing things that not many others would get to witness in a lifetime of memories. I would encounter Spirits of Ghosts and other wild beings. As well as even the myths and legends of the woods themselves.

Sasquatch for the fact of the matter. I would have multiple encounters while being out in the woods fishing and or hunting. But for the most part my family and I would see and have many accounts of coming close to and as well crossing the paths with spirits of the past. Who had passed and hadn't found their way to the light so to speak.

Or maybe they were just visiting for a few moments. However their were so many different interactions that they couldn't all be explained away. Not so easily anyway for that matter. Since I could remember all of these wild things started once I'd started school. My local town of Norwood, Ohio. A beautiful but mystical place on the map of the United States.

The town had been built with not much thought I had guessed. Since most of it had been constructed on or near the location of the Hopewell Indian Tribe. They had called this land their home since well before we had arrived at a much later date. At the upper elevations of my home town. Sat a monster load of homes. That had been built near Hopewell serpent mounds.

(Chapter 2)

At night growing up we could see weird lights all about the woods. As we would play hide and seek at night. Very strange things occurred up on the top of that small mountain. Their was a Nickname that had been given to the particular set of forest. Indian Mound was what I had k own it to be called as I grew up.

I had witnessed so many things in that set of woods. A sighting of a Sasquatch while on the way home from school. Their had always been a feeling that overcame me while in those woods. It was never a calm and peaceful feeling. But just the opposite of that feeling. It was totally different than the feeling I got while roaming any other section of woods.

It seemed that their was always something going on in our section of town. My friends and I lived just 500 feet from the woods. We were the closet out of all of the towns people. We also had the most wild experiences that would happen to us often. Spirits and or Ghosts would seem to play games with us at night.

We learned to deal with the spirits over the years. The hauntings if they could be classed as that. Became so routine that it just became a thing. Nothing more nothing less. In the end we just took it in spiritually that they were just trying to communicate with us in anyway they could do so. Drawers opening often during the night. Spoons and forks flying off of the kitchen table.

At random, as if it weren't nothing to us when it would happen. There was always a glow that seemed to radiate from the forest at night. Giving it a wild but beautiful look to it. To scary to go in on nights when that had occurred. It came to be so scary that we quit going in the woods and started playing block tag down on the streets of the city itself.

(Chapter 3)

Even when we stopped playing block tag in the woods. While we were down off of the mountain I seemed to have the feeling of being watched from up above. From up on the hill it felt as of eyes were on me the whole time. And that was no joke, I kept an uneasy feeling wherever it would he that I still had eyes upon me from the hill.

The only time I felt at ease while living on that side of town was during the day. But still I would feel as if I were still being watched. Even then and I found that to be so damn odd feeling. It overwhelmed me at times. I could never figure it out over the years just what it was that would cause that intense of a feeling. Did I have a connection of some kind to this place.

I was starting to feel as if I were linked to this place in some sort of way. It just felt as if I were always being drawn in to that set of woods even when I would be away from them. It was not a normal feeling at all for me. But what I hadn't known at that direct time. Was that I had been born a twin. I hadn't a clue at the time and wouldn't know until a later date.

And even after I had learned that I had been born in fact a twin and an identical one as well. It would still take years to before I was able to put all of the clues together. And come to realize it was the special set of circumstances. That had given me all of the special gifts that were most likely needed. In order to have the chance to experience all of the great things that I would hear and see during my lifetime.

So many incidents that would not only shock me but also scare me as well. I would learn very fast that in our world their was such a thing as Spirits and Ghosts. And other strange creatures out there living among us. It really is all about timing when it comes down to having an encounter. With something that is not of this world or Is of this world and not a confirmed species as of yet.

(Chapter 4)

I will never forget the night that I stayed all night wIth a good friend of mine. A friend who had only lived several houses down from me. But I stayed there more than at home. I did this because my father was a bad Alcoholic. And to escape the abuse I'd just stay elsewhere to not have to suffer the torment. It was always a Friday when I'd head out for the weekend.

My best friend and I Ronald Ledbetter had fun on the weekends. We would watch movies or M.T.V. and jam out all weekend. We would call girls and make prank calls to other friends as well. It was so much fun staying away from home. But late at night was scary at the Ledbetter household. You would start to hear things moving about.

The doors would start to open allover the house for no apparent reason. The stairs would start to sound as if someone were coming up to the second floor. But we were already in bed all of us who were staying there. It wasn't that scary most of the time. But when we would hear sounds from the third floor attic when Noone was home but us was totally frightening.

There were other times when we would hear conversations that were happening down on the first floor. But everyone was up on the second floor sleeping. Those were scary moments as well also. The house was haunted to say the very least. But not the only haunted house I'd experience in my life. Their would come way worse.

In my first years of Junior High School I dated a young girl named Star Smart. She was in to the new Gothic type phase some had gotten into as of lately. She was still amazingly beautiful and I was into her heavy. She lived in a huge wild home in the middle of town. A huge Red brick home. Red candles in every window of the home burned on a nightly basis.

(Chapter 5)

We would go to her house after school and smoke pot usually most days And make out sessions would occur as well. We had fun back in those days. But I remember one night the topic came up about breaking out a Ouija board. I instantly declined to be any part of it. I had already been warned about the weakening of spirits by my Aunt Brenda.

She warned me as a young kid never to allow anyone to put me into that type of predicament. So I made sure I let it be known the dangers of what was being brought about in this situation. I told everyone there that it was super dangerous to summon the dead spirits with the Ouija board. Noone listened to me as they were all stoned to the bone at the time.

Once night had fallen the alcohol was opened up and the candles were lit up all around the house. Then the board itself was broke out of its box. As the group set up at the table. Laying down a table cloth to enable the board to stay in one spot. Everyone sat down in a chair as Star sat down as well. Telling everyone to stay put if anything freaky happened.

That it would most likely upset any spirit that may show up during the weakening of the spirits. As the group sat at the table Star began asking questions. Are there any spirits among us tonight. Over and over she asked again and again. After a 15 minute window her hands started to move the board around in circles. Spelling out the answer yes to her question.

Then she asked who was with us in the room. Nothing happened for a few minutes. Then out of nowhere the board started to move yet once again on its own. Spelling out the word demon. Then in that moment the curtains in the room blew straight out as if the wind had blown hard through the window. The problem was that the windows were shut.

(Chapter 6)

The moment made for a very scary situation. Everyone yelled out in fear as the curtains fell finally back towards their former positions. I told everyone to stop freaking out. As I once again asked Star to stop with this reading on the board. I told her I was afraid someone could get hurt in the process. Of course she didn't listen to me as she continued to do her thing.

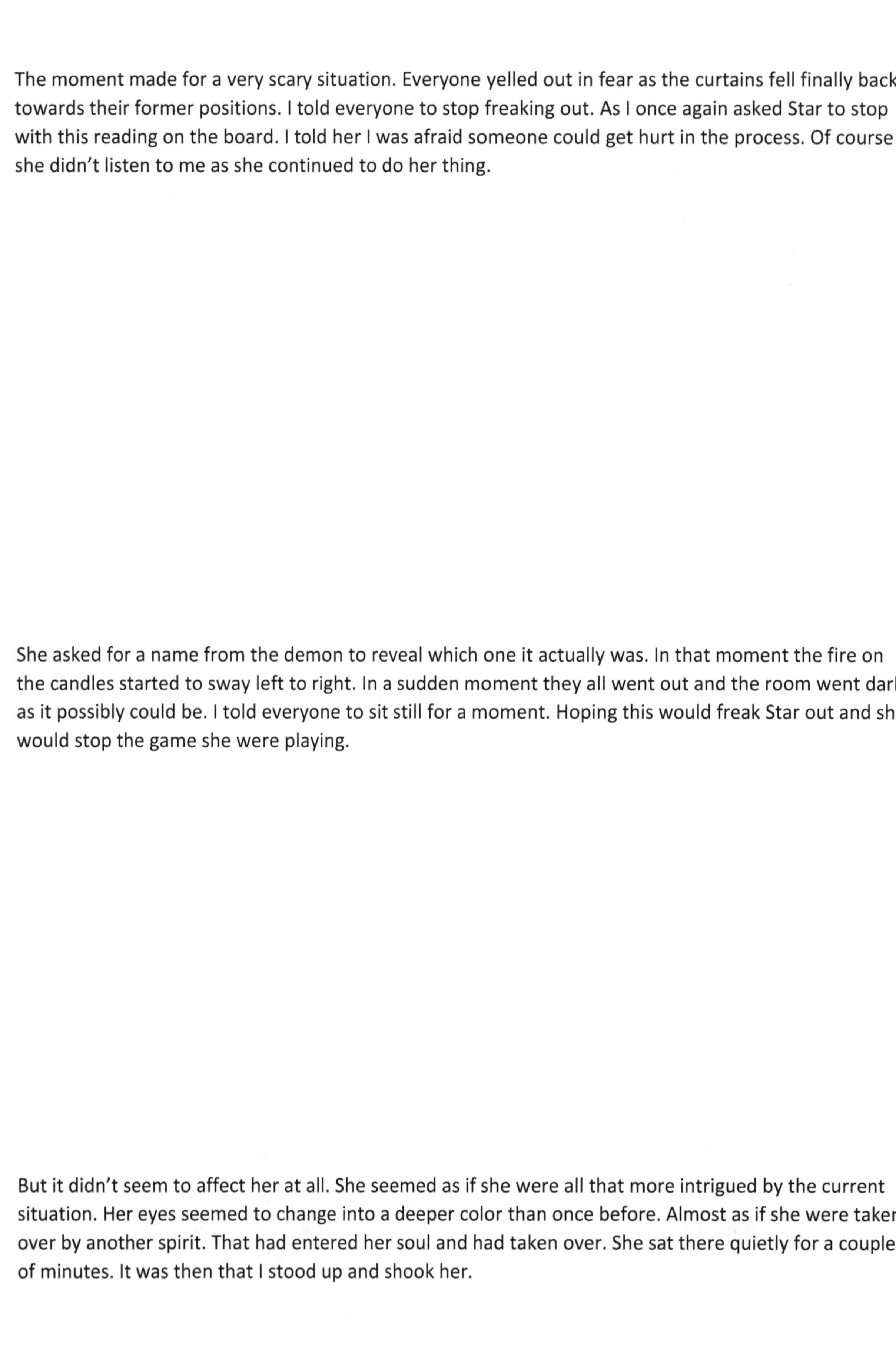

She asked for a name from the demon to reveal which one it actually was. In that moment the fire on the candles started to sway left to right. In a sudden moment they all went out and the room went dark as it possibly could be. I told everyone to sit still for a moment. Hoping this would freak Star out and she would stop the game she were playing.

But it didn't seem to affect her at all. She seemed as if she were all that more intrigued by the current situation. Her eyes seemed to change into a deeper color than once before. Almost as if she were taken over by another spirit. That had entered her soul and had taken over. She sat there quietly for a couple of minutes. It was then that I stood up and shook her.

She finally came about and asked me what I was doing. That it was very dangerous for me to touch her while she were possessed by a spirit. It was then that I stepped towards the door opening out into the hallway. As I walked over towards it the door began to close slowly. As if a spirit had pushed it lightly to close before I got through the opening.

As I got to the door it had closed all of the way. And now I found myself struggling to open the door. It felt as if someone or something on the other side of the door was holding it shut. Keeping me from getting through it and out into the hallway and then out of the house itself. I was starting to have fear come over me in that moment.

(Chapter 7)

I yelled out for Star to put up the Ouija Board immediately. And told her the door was being held shut by a spirit or something of the sort. She refused to listen as she continued to ask questions. I stormed over to the table once again. Grabbing the board and tool from her hand. And folded it and put both pieces back into the box. As I did I slung it into the far corner as if it were a bowling ball.

As it slid I walked back over towards the door. As I grabbed it and turned the knob the door finally opened. I told everyone to go to hell as I walked out into the hallway. I stepped out of the house in an instant. As I did I looked up towards the front windows. As I did I see a wicked thing happen. Each candle sitting in each separate window had lit back up.

And I knew for sure right then and there that this house was definetly haunted. Their was no doubt in my mind at all. I broke up with Star that very same night. And hardly ever talked to her again after that night. It was when I knew the rumors had been right. She had most likely studied some sort of Black Magic. Or Witchcraft. I couldn't allow that in my life.

I had enough of that already going on in my life. As my father had been having an affair with a woman who studied Black Magic herself. And I felt as if our family was Cursed already by a spell of some sort. That had been placed upon us by the woman. We had suffered some awful bad luck since the two of them had started having an affair with one another.

I just wanted all of the shit that was going on to stop. We had suffered so much as of late it felt surreal. The passing of not only my Aunt Brenda. But the passing of my Uncle Chris also. Followed by myself getting struck by a baseball in mouth. That had knocked me out as well as setting all of my teeth loose. The pain had been unbearable for a few weeks. Not letting up It had been so hard to rest in anyway .

(Chapter 8)

Now I had already seen a dentist over the issue. And had been cleared to play ball once again. It was then that I met my future wife to be. It would be the middle of the summer time. And swimming in our local river would be a daily experience. On my birthday it had been one helluva day. A very hot day it was that day. We were night swimming when I had become caught in fishing line.

I lost my air and had taken on water into my lungs. And soon after I had lost my consciousness. I remembered as my soul had started to fade from body. The light started to come over my body. As I finally had come back away from the light. I woke up back at the river. A good friend had saved life by working on me. Giving me C.P.R. until I expelled the water from my lungs.

As I came to I remember back to them carrying me up over their heads. The whole group had me and were not letting me go. Trying to get me to safety once again. They had me and weren't going to lose me at any cost what so ever. I'm forever in their debt for that night long ago. I also lost my virginity that very same night also.

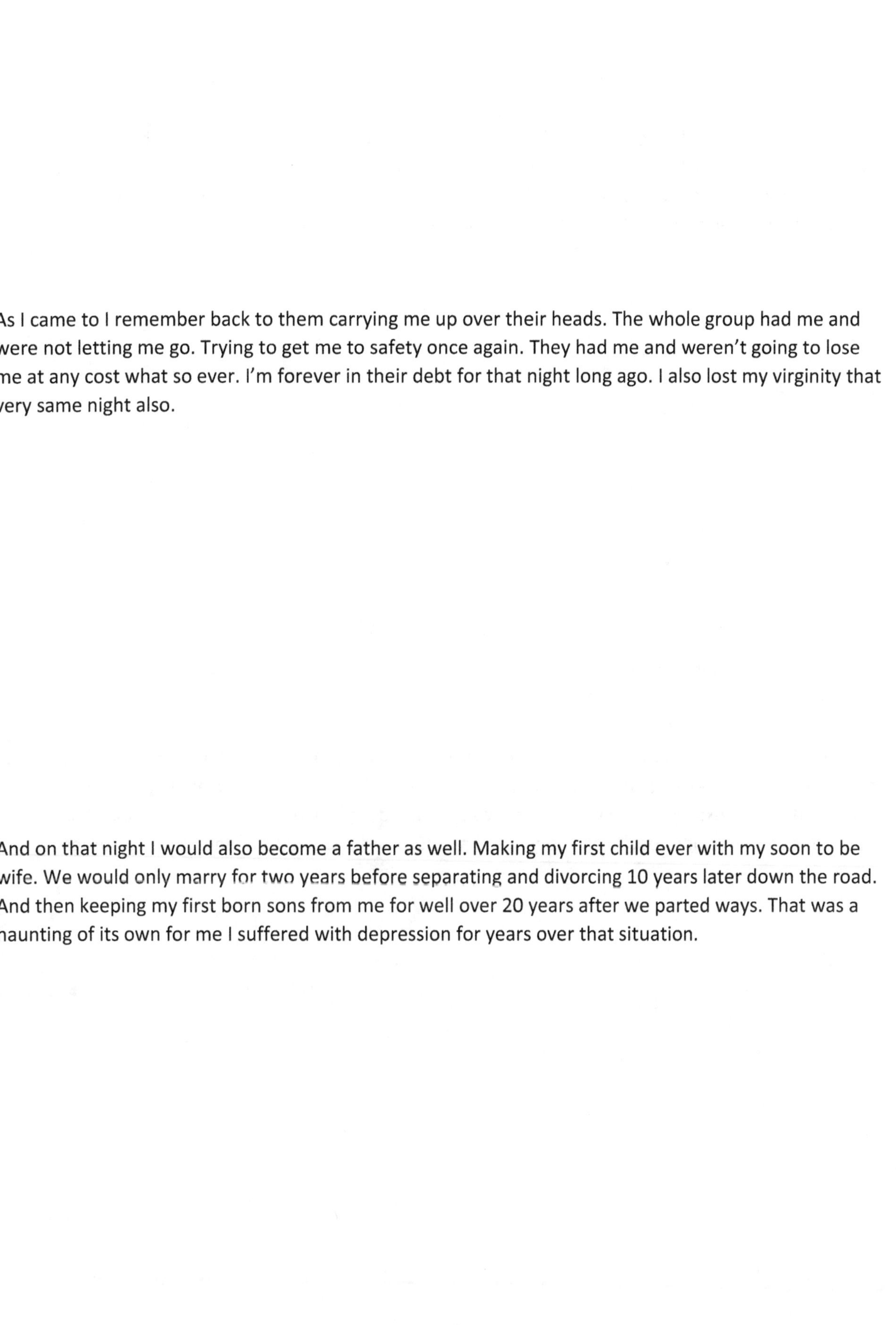

And on that night I would also become a father as well. Making my first child ever with my soon to be wife. We would only marry for two years before separating and divorcing 10 years later down the road. And then keeping my first born sons from me for well over 20 years after we parted ways. That was a haunting of its own for me I suffered with depression for years over that situation.

She would also hire my divorce lawyer after not showing up for our divorce hearing. Which was another haunting of it's own. Making that particular move to be the plaintiff on the case itself. Such a series of dirty and unprofessional events that would take place in my life. I should have sued honestly for those very moves but I would let the lord handle that for me.

(Chapter 9)

I've been blessed in many ways in life as well as Cursed over my years on this earth. I've seen everything from U.F.O.'s to two separate Bigfoot sightings also. Both of them very close up enough to say without a doubt. That I know exactly what I seen those two separate days. Since I've put out my stories about what I've seen. My phones each and every one that I purchase seemed to be monitored by others.

I've not put everything out there all in one book. I split all of my happenings up and put them all into different books. So it's not all put into one long story. And I can look back and remember everything in better detail. There are so any forgotten incidents as well. And I get aggravated about not being able to reflect on all of my wild incidents.

The ones I remember though are still very frightening as hell to me. That is why I never forget them I guess the reason would be. So many nights while I was out fishing and would see strange things out in the wilderness. Things that couldn't be explained at all. Rocks being thrown at me while fishing. Strange lights up in the sky. Strange objects roaming about our skies as well also.

Some of them occuring even in the daytime as well. Cigar shaped objects and many other formed shapes all in one area as if they were in a defensive position. There are other forms of life that live in our world that are without a doubt among us. I've known this since I was old enough to know better. I have had hauntings in more than just a few places where I resided as a kid growing up.

In several homes we lived in we'd experience voices mumbling lightly in the night hours. Doors opening and closing during the night also. My father often had stories of seeing the grim reaper on more than one occasion. Once while choking on a sandwich. And another time while he'd had alcohol poisoning from Alcohol consumption.

(Chapter 10)

I've had many lights turn on and off in many home that I grew up in over the years I've been alive. I've also had so many television sets that would go off and on as well. Freaking me out to the point of running out of the house. Many knocks at doors on certain nights would also occur. Often when Noone was home but myself. Scary to say the least.

I have had incidents where things on tables would just fly off for no reason at all. I feel as if I were born just to experience all of these super natural encounters with things of the unknown. Myths and legends of many kinds. Not sure if it had anything to do with me being an identical twin. Or if it was because I had a pure and living soul compared to others.

Something was going on with my life I could start to tell at an early age. In all honesty by the time I'd hit my teenage years I knew I was one of the gifted ones. It was when I had started to experience De-Ja-Vu mixed in with everything else I was already experiencing in my life. Better and more intense incidents would start to take place.

It was when we moved out of Norwood and into Reading, Ohio. It started before we even moved in to the house. My little Brother Jason Lilly had went over to install some new carpet. He went alone and was all by himself that first night. He arrived and went in and turned on the lights. Once he had retrieved all of the equipment to lay the new carpet it started to unfold.

He told me that he had gone into the very back room. Furthest away from the back door when it had hit the fan. He was bent over and unrolling the material when something from behind had taken its finger and wiped it as hard as possible up his ass Crack and up his back to his neck in a split seconds time. He froze with fear in that moment.

(Chapter 11)

As he dropped his carpentry knife to the floor he took off running out of the house. He grabbed his phone to male a call but decided not to make any call at all. He didn't want to freak anyone else out. Figuring if he told anyone there wouldn't be a move at all. So he decided to go back in and start once again. He stepped into the house once more.

Hoping that whatever had just happened didn't happen again. But only a few minutes would pass before the spirit would interact with him yet again. As Jason leaned over to reach for his phone to answer a call. His phone automatically had turned off. Out of nowhere the power on his cell phone had been zapped. Freaking Jay out yet again.

It was in that moment that the same exact thing happened once again. The feeling of a huge finger had felt Jason up. From the Crack of his ass all the way up his spine and to the back of his neck. He immediately jumped up and an out of the house again. Totally flipping out in this moment. He wasn't sure if he wanted to allow his family to move into this house.

But the fact of the matter was that the family had nowhere else to go to. They had searched for this place on an emergency basis. In desperate need of a place to move to and call home. So he realized that their really wasn't a choice in the matter. The family had to move here for atleast a month or two. The plan would be to save up and then move again.

Jason waited until the next morning before he went back in the house. He made sure he had someone with him when he did go back their. The work would be finished within the next two days. And the move would be made on a Friday evening. As they started moving the furniture into the U-Haul the snow started to fall very heavily as the wind picked up.

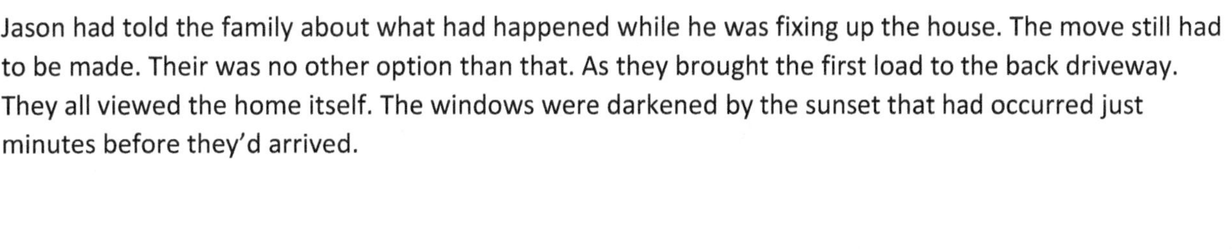

Jason had told the family about what had happened while he was fixing up the house. The move still had to be made. Their was no other option than that. As they brought the first load to the back driveway. They all viewed the home itself. The windows were darkened by the sunset that had occurred just minutes before they'd arrived.

(Chapter 12)

Their was a weird feeling that overcame the whole family. As they all described the homes built in features. They backed the truck up the driveway and parked it right before the garage. At the back steps leading into the kitchen. Everyone got out and started to unload the U-Haul of its contents. As the family went in to take a look.

They all suddenly felt uneasy as if something were off. As they traveled from room to room they got to see the fine wood work that had been done in the building of the home. The upstairs was layed out with Cherry and Walnut wood. The trim was beautiful as well as the huge walking closets that had been constructed by the carpenters of the past.

Two in total enormous closets with so much space it could almost be used as a spare bedroom if need be. To the right side of the room was another huge set of built in drawers made out of Walnut wood. Dark and beautifully layed out and into the wall. Which was really odd to see. Then Jeff noticed a secret door that opened just a little bit.

He swung it open to see another huge room that had been constructed as well. This house is very unique the whole family agreed on that with no doubt. They slowly made their way back down and into the back bedrooms of the home. Jason pointed out the room in which he were assaulted by a spirit. That had everyone uneasy at the moment.

Then they made their way down into the basement. It was also layed out just as the rest of the house was. Their was a bar built off to the side of the room. In the center of the room was a huge fireplace. That could damn well near hold a half a cord of wood at once. In the back of the room was a washer and dryer set. And a back door that led up and into the back yard.

Their also was a huge garage off to the side of the yard as well. The yard itself was big enough to hold a pool and a horse shoe pit. As well as a corn hole set as well. Fenced in all the way around and secure. Good for the dogs Jason said and everyone agreed to that also. The move would be finished by 12 midnight. And everyone would finally set up to get some sleep.

(Chapter 13)

Nothing happened that first night. Not for quite a while would they start to experience anything out of the ordinary. But one day Jason brought over his new girlfriend to meet the family. As Christina came into the kitchen to meet everyone she had a weird look on her face. "Wow" she said, "the energy in this house is wild'. "Did anyone check on the history of this house". "Especially before you all moved in" she asked.

Jason answered Christina immediately. "Well hello no" he replied, "we didn't have any time to check on that". Christina broke out her phone in that moment. "Were in luck" she said. "I have a built in Ghost App on my phone". She turned her phone on and went straight to the Ghost App. Turning it on we all heard in an instant the beeps going off.

"I knew it" Christina said. "There is something in this house". And it wants to communicate she told the family. The device kept beeping stronger as she headed through the hallway. Towards the back bedroom the beeping became faster. As Christina walked back out of the bedroom she put the device on the closet door. The beeps turned into a long drawn out noise. "This is it" she said.

Christina opened the hallway door and froze immediately. "Something happened in this closet or this house" she shouted. Shutting the door in an instant. She took in one deep long breath. As if she'd been frightened to death by something as she opened the door to the closet itself. "Well it's time to hit the library" Christina said. " I've got some things to check out in the local archives".

She looked at Jason and they both made a move towards the back kitchen door. That would lead them to her car that was parked in the driveway. "We Will be back in a little while" she said to the family. "I'm going to find out just what it was" , that happened here she told her knew kin. As the car started and she and Jason left for the library.

She made her way to the town library and parked her car upon going in. She told her new boyfriend that their definetly was some sort of spiritual being that was residing in their new home. They both jumped out of the car and walked in the building. Jumping on the archive machine. Christina began scrolling through the old news paper clippings.

(Chapter 14)

And there it was, right in front of her face. An old newspaper article. A middle aged man had been found in the home. The authorities had found him dead. Hanging from inside of the hallway closet. When he was found, their was a stack of brand new cell phones beneath his feet upon their entry. That immediately freaked Christina and Jason both out.

It was in that moment they both knew that the house they'd moved into was most likely without any doubts at all haunted. She read the rest of the article. As it said that the scene did look suspicious and that the police had left the investigation open on this exact case. The man was known to have ties to a local drug ring.

Jason and Christina both looked to one another as they both finished reading the article. They had to go back and tell the rest of the family about what they had just learned. But first Christina wanted to check a little deeper into the houses history. To see of anything else bad had happened there. And sure enough their was more to be learned.

Their had been a young wife who had died in the home as well. Shortly after getting married she had become ill. And had passed in the home shortly after moving in. That startled the two of them immensely as they read through to the finish. Jason was feeling guilty in that moment. He had moved his kin into this home. Without checking its history first.

He knew that his family was stuck there for at the very least a couple of months time. And it would be a rough ass couple of months to say the least. A few weeks would pass with no troubles. But then it started. The first thing that had happened was almost as if it were a warning of what was yet to come.

(Chapter 15)

One day while outside painting the house. Jeff had been on the back side of the house painting the shutters on the lower windows. When out of nowhere he looked up only to see a white woman in a wedding dress. Staring at him down below her. He immediately jumped down off of the ladder. Running up the stairs to the upper bedrooms.

Only to find Noone there at all in the back room. Jeff was shocked at what he'd seen just moments earlier. When all of a sudden out of nowhere the doorbell rang. Jeff walked down the steps and answered the door. But Noone was there. Then he remembered what he'd noticed upon moving in.

The door bell had been disconnected from the electrical supply long ago. He was frozen with fear in that moment. Not knowing what was happening was putting him on high alert at the moment. He walked back into the kitchen and took a seat for a few minutes. Trying to explain to himself rationally, what just had happened.

None of It could be explained in any way shape or form. It was definetly a ghost of some kind playing games once again. Trying to communicate or just letting the family know that it was present in the home still. Jeff didn't know if this was a territorial thing or just the opposite of that. The question now was how long would all of this continue to go on.

For some reason deep down in his gut Jeff knew this was only just the beginning. A strange feeling now overwhelmed him in that moment of time. He was distraught and angry as well. Wondering why this was happening to his family. They had all just moved back home. And were once again a full family. Life had brought them all back together again.

(Chapter 16)

They had all been pitching in and taking care of their father once again. He had suffered several deep strokes 15 years back. And was still a paraplegic. Needing very much attention in a 24 hour basis. Now the threat of possibly evil spirits dwelled over the family. The years prior to this hadn't been all to kind to them as well. Constant struggles and pain and agony from death surrounded them.

Just when they thought they could get passed it all and make a fresh start. This would happen go figure. It just wasn't in the cards for this family to have any peace. Nothing more than a daily struggle to survive. That was all this family knew and had known for many years now. They had learned how to get through anything together. And now this situation had came along.

Jason sat his mother down and had a talk with her later on that night. Promising her that a move would be made within a month no more than that. And it wouldn't he long until they had peace possibly for first time in a very long time. He had been eyeing a house just a couple of streets down the road. Not to far from where they were now.

His other just smiled at him. As if it didn't matter at all to her whether they stayed or went. It was in that moment she had just given up on all of it. Nothing mattered except the fact that she had finally gotten out of the horrible city shed suffered in for so long. She had found peace after all of these years finally.

She had decided to just make a good it right where she was at now. Wherever the journey would take her shed kindly except it and run with it. She had learned how to adjust over the years. Weeks later more family would move in. As Jason would move his two girls into the house with the rest of the family. Their rooms would be upstairs from their mama and papaw.

Chapter 17

For some reason when the move was made to Maple Drive. The whole family would end up staying there together. Every room would eventually be filled by a member of the family. Even the basement had became a bedroom at the end of it all. Jason would end up staying down their with Onyx. His new pit bull that had been given to him. All I know is that my brother was of sound mind when he and that dog were united.

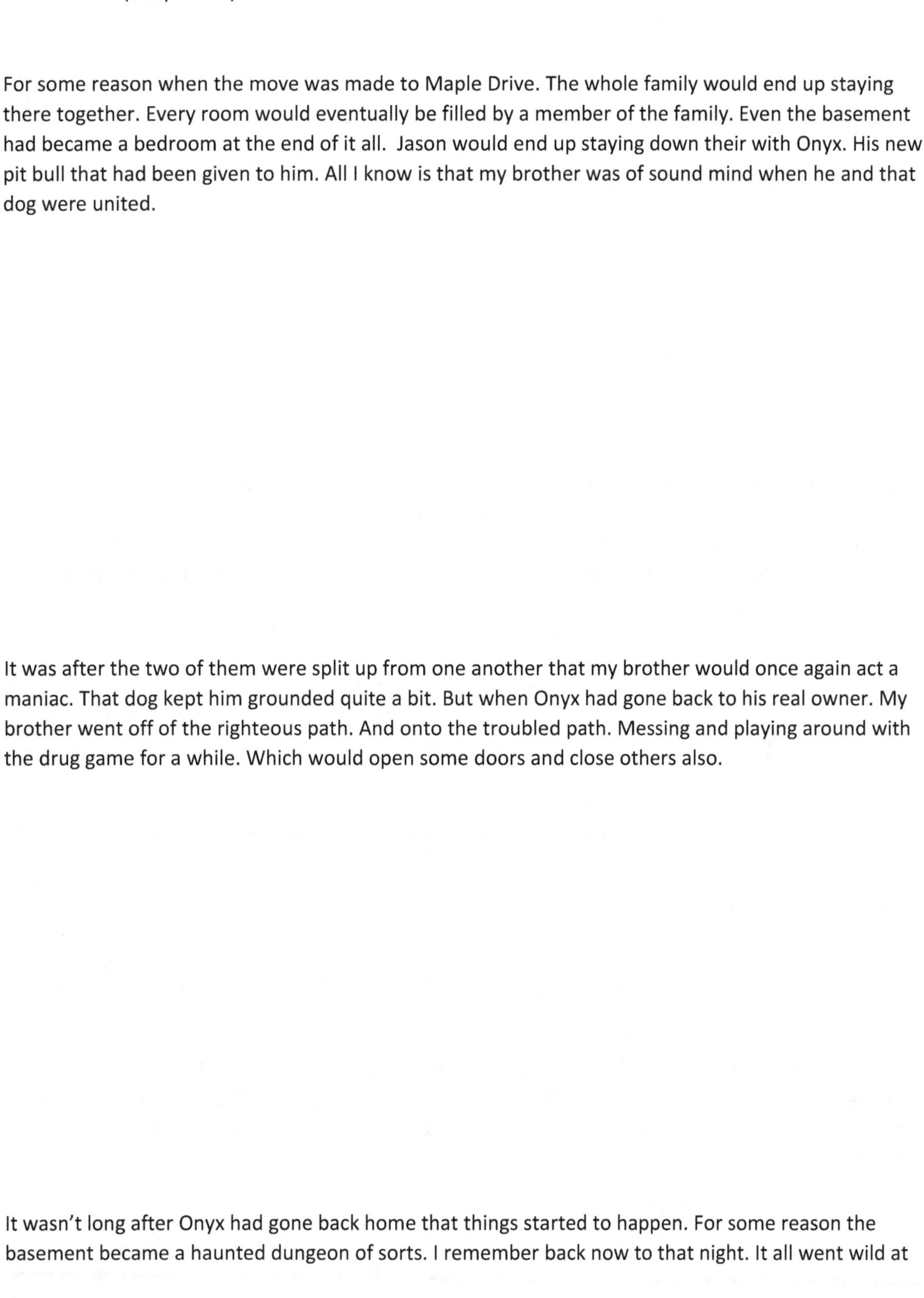

It was after the two of them were split up from one another that my brother would once again act a maniac. That dog kept him grounded quite a bit. But when Onyx had gone back to his real owner. My brother went off of the righteous path. And onto the troubled path. Messing and playing around with the drug game for a while. Which would open some doors and close others also.

It wasn't long after Onyx had gone back home that things started to happen. For some reason the basement became a haunted dungeon of sorts. I remember back now to that night. It all went wild at about 2:00 Am. Jason came flying up out of the basement as white as a ghost. And I'd never seen him move that fast in my life ever. Like the wind he flew up those basement stairs.

Saying he had heard noises from the back of the basement while he was sleeping. When he was finally awaken from all of the noises. What he seen was not of this earth. A demon that had the legs of a huge goat and a set of immense wings that were the shape and form as that of a bat were spread out. The face was so horrifying he only got a glimpse of it. But that alone was well more than enough to terrify him.

Once it had been seen it fled in behind the washer and dryer and then disappeared into thin air. My brother had never been more scared in his life. The next day he moved out of the basement and down the street to the new house. After begging the owner to allow them to move early. Upon leaving he took our mother and our father as well with him.

(Chapter 18)

Leaving the only two who were left at the house that day was Chad and myself. We weren't welcome to do the move with our family. Jason and I didn't get along to well at that time. We had two different opinions on how life was supposed to be lived. He lived in the fast lane. And I lived in the slow lane. But I also was a giver and a helper. As he was a taker flat out at that time.

He would change later on down the road before his passing. But at this time he was in a different mind set all together. He was kind of evil himself and mean towards others back in those days. The transition was made and we all split up once again. Then the shit really hit the fan. At night Chad would sleep in his room off to the left from the hallway. The other room had been abandoned.

I myself made the kitchen my room during the night. Just so I could protect the house from whoever may try to break in or harm us. It was the very beginning of the drug epidemic. And times were getting tough. Theft and stealing was already through the roof in our new city. It was on a Saturday night when the next incident had taken place. First the doorbell went off at Midnight once again.

It woke me immediately and I hit the door as fast as a lightning bolt. To see if anyone was really there. But when I opened the door not a soul was present. I knew then it was the spirits or the demons yet again. Then at about 2:00 Am once again Chad and I were awaken by something moving about in the basement once again. We both thought about the demon Jason had described seeing.

That really frightened us a whole hell of a lot at the time. It sounded as if a bat were loose and couldn't find its way out. After about 20 minutes the sounds stopped all at once. About 3 days later I was up in the girls old room playing the PlayStation when I went to sit on a milk crate in the corner of the room. When I went to sit there was a horrible sound behind my back.

A sound of what seemed to be that of a wild rabid dog. Who had contacted rabies and had gone mad. It was the scariest sound I'd ever heard to this day. Even the sounds I'd heard while in the woods weren't this scary. I was shaken so badly that I didn't go up their ever again. Not even to grab left over possessions that were ours. They were left to whomever needed them.

(Chapter 19)

The house became more and more haunted over the next few days. The atmosphere had definetly changed and it could be felt just by sitting inside the home itself. You could cut the energy with a knife. It was rather difficult to deal with to say the least. But we dealt with it by listening to music and drugs and alcohol seemed to help us along our journey.

But those things only helped for a limited amount of time. Once it had gotten late into the night hours. The spirits that roamed our house would be heard for sure. Norther how loud the noise. I remember one night the stereo was so loud. Then out of nowhere from upstairs we'd heard the loudest bang in quite sometime. Jolting us from our seats.

It had to be the demon once again. And it was highly upset by the music that was being played. But it was the only way we could drown out all of the sounds we were hearing all about the house. There was more than one spirit in the house now for sure. And they were all letting us know that they were now present That was the scariest part of the whole ordeal.

The next morning at noon on the dot the doorbell rang again. And then we heard crashing around in the basement once again. The spirits were roused up for sure. I felt they were trying to push us out of the home all together. These particular spirits were particularly upset in a huge way. And were now lashing out in short but savage moments.

The constant banging that went on all about the house was starting to become exhausting in a major way. Very few hours of sleep my brother and I both had in over a weeks time was wearing us down quickly. I had made a huge fire in the basement fireplace purposely. To try and stir up and arouse the demons once again.

(Chapter 20)

It was on a Sunday that my brother had brought us up a litter of 5 baby pit bulls. He wanted us to take care of for a few weeks. We were totally frightened for their safety. Chad placed them in a closet in his bedroom. He would be the protector of the litter until they were ready to go to their new homes. What happened later was so damn traumatic.

We woke up one morning to find all 5 pit bull puppies dead. We were so sad and crying. As we placed them each in a towel to take outside to bury them we both cried. Mad and also sad as well. We couldn't believe that this had happened. Why would anything target an animal ? It didn't make any sense at all to us. We picked the pups up and started to carry them out side when the chimer on the clock went off once again.

The shocking part was that the clock hadn't worked in years. Their were no batteries in it so we knew something was present again with us. We stepped outside and buried the dogs next to the house. In a 3 foot hole to keep them safe from other animals. When we finished we stepped back in the house and just like that we heard more movement in the basement.

It was loud and powerful whatever it was that was down their moving about. And upstairs was starting to pop off again. All of a sudden I heard a noise and went to check it out. When I got to the set of stairs leading up to the second floor. I look up towards the second floor and their it started to appear. The deep scratches going across the wooden closet doors.

It was so loud that Chad had heard it from the kitchen. We both ran out of the house at that moment. Things were becoming un-hinged inside our home. We were not wanted there any longer that was for sure. But we didn't want to leave. This was our home , we had just moved in less than a month earlier.

(Chapter 21)

The battle to keep our home would continue for at the least a few more days. The spirits and or demons that had been present with us. Each day had become more and more violent. The days would become more and more frightening as they came. The noises would grow louder with each and every single encounter that happened. More intense also they'd become from one on to the next.

Very scary the situation had become for my brother and I both. We were set on staying but, the spirits were not going to have any of that at all. They were dead set on not getting us out. And not allowing us to stay for good. The next incident would occur as I woke up early one morning and had started to make my coffee. I walked into the kitchen and forgotten my phone in the living room.

As I walked back into the living room. I looked over towards the stairs leading up to the second floor. When I saw as plain as day the woman in the wedding dress heading up the steps one by one as she made her way to the second floor. It was then that I found myself fleeing towards the back door and out of the house yet once again.

Chad still asleep in his bedroom didn't have a clue what had just happened to me. I stayed outside for about 20 minutes in the rain. Before heading back into the house to make my coffee. The hauntings were getting more intense as the moments passed by. I just had an overwhelming feeling take over me once again. Not being able to shake them this time.

We would get frequent visits from Jason and Christina. They would come to check up on us. Making sure we were OK. And upon entering the house they both would freak out a bit. Christina would have goose bumps on her arms. You could see them as plain as day. As she would say. "WOW" their getting stronger aren't they ? As I would immediately agree " with her "Yes".

(Chapter 22)

Jason and Christina left immediately the house. Out of fear that their presence in the home would aggravate the spirits that were already present and letting their madness be known. The rest of that day would go uneventful for the most part. The spirits could only show their madness for a while. Before they would run out of energy.

Then they would have to lay dormant until they could once again build up their energy. And once that had happened they could torment the family yet again once more. It was basically a standoff that was going down for the home itself. To see who was more determined to keep the house in their grasp. The demons and evil spirits against myself and the ghost of the wedding woman in the white dress.

It was a couple days later when my brother Chad and myself. Had started to hear what sounded like hooves walking around up on the second floor bedrooms. It was then that we both became terrified of what that just might be. Not long after those sounds had started to occur. My brother said I love you Jeff but, I've got to go. As he packed his clothes as fast as he could and walked out of the front door.

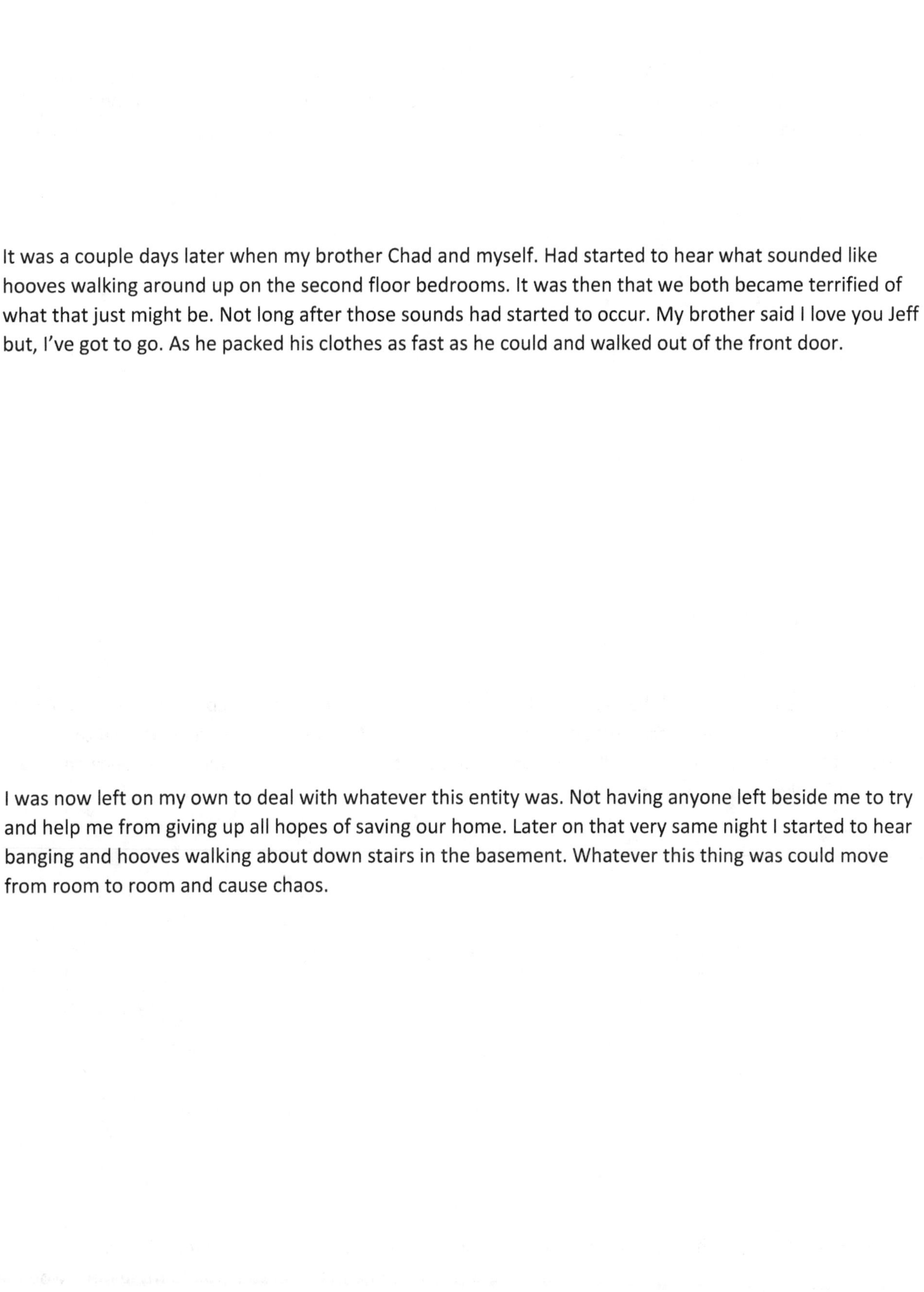

I was now left on my own to deal with whatever this entity was. Not having anyone left beside me to try and help me from giving up all hopes of saving our home. Later on that very same night I started to hear banging and hooves walking about down stairs in the basement. Whatever this thing was could move from room to room and cause chaos.

I was scared to death at this time. I had the Bible right in my hand. Sleeping with it on a nightly basis. In hopes that it and it alone would help keep safe. From the demon that now haunted our home on Maple Drive to the fullest of its capabilities. And it had grown even stronger. I would hear stuff being moved. And the demon would bang on the closet doors also.

(Chapter 23)

I had never been more scared than I was at this moment in time. Our house had become the stomping grounds for evil spirits. I had been battling them with the Bible. Constantly saying prayers, and the reading of the book of Psalms as well. To try and push the demons from out of our home. Once and for all, so my family could come home again.

But that wasn't going to happen in any way. They had now set their claws into the foundation so to speak. And they weren't going to let go of it. I was at my wits end in this battle I found myself in. I would get phone calls every few hours. Checking in on me to see if I were still alive. My family had become so rattled by these events.

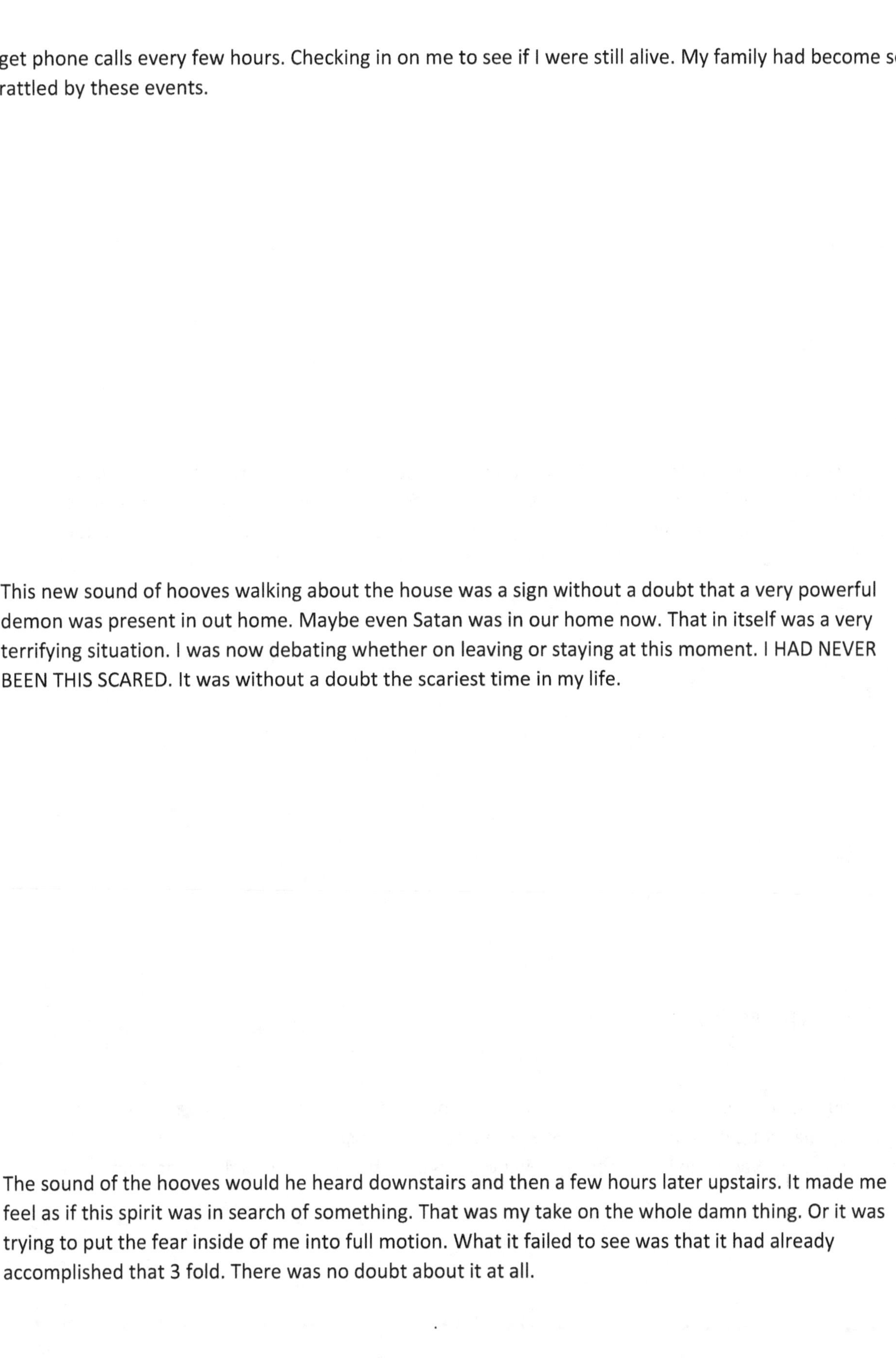

This new sound of hooves walking about the house was a sign without a doubt that a very powerful demon was present in out home. Maybe even Satan was in our home now. That in itself was a very terrifying situation. I was now debating whether on leaving or staying at this moment. I HAD NEVER BEEN THIS SCARED. It was without a doubt the scariest time in my life.

The sound of the hooves would he heard downstairs and then a few hours later upstairs. It made me feel as if this spirit was in search of something. That was my take on the whole damn thing. Or it was trying to put the fear inside of me into full motion. What it failed to see was that it had already accomplished that 3 fold. There was no doubt about it at all.

I was now debating on whether to pack it up and roll on out or stay and try to get my hands on some holy water. I've a Quick call to Christina and asked her to go to the nearest church and try to get some water blessed for me. Then I would try to say quotes from the Bible myself. As I sprinkled out Holy Water 8n order to rid our house of the spirits who now called our house their home.

(Chapter 24)

The errand was run and the water was brought to the house. Shortly after being blessed by the church itself. Christina brought in the blessed contents in a box and left shortly after she'd arrived. The plan was on and I now was alone in the house allover once again. I broke out the Holy water from its container.

I then reached for the Bible as I opened it up to the book of Psalms. Reading verse after verse as I entered each room. Sprinkling a little of the blessed liquid of the Lord onto the floor. Then I waited for a while to see what if any good had came from this process what so ever. And for a couple days I heard nothing at all. Not a sound one from anything out of the ordinary.

It was about a week later that everything exploded. On a dark and snowy night at about 3 am I was awaken by the most God awful whine. This cry or whine was the most wicked noise I'd ever heard. It was if something had came back from the dead. Or was dying, one or the other it was so frightening at the time. It had came from down in the basement.

Then it just stopped out of nowhere. As I shook in total fear for my life. I started to look around the 2nd
floor rooms for evidence of any spiritual connection. Each closet had several items that had belonged to
kids. Setting dead center in the middle of each room itself. That to me was very weird. Nothing
happened for the rest of that night.

Then after a few days it started allover again. At midnight as always the sounds could be heard from the
basement. Then at about 2 am sounds of hooves could be heard upstairs as well. Followed by knocks on
the closet doors. There was no way I was going upstairs in the darkness. I felt if I did I wouldn't ever
come back down again. Not alive atleast anyway.

(Chapter 25)

It felt to me as of something was trying to lure me to a set room at a set time each night. So I would just choose to move to the exact opposite in which the situation was occuring. That seemed to have been the correct choice that I'd made. Steering clear of the evil apparitions that now were controlling the house. I couldn't believe this was happening to me.

Me. Was now wondering if this was all because of me or someone else. Or if it were linked to the dead man that had been found in the hallway closet. Shortly before we'd moved in their. It weighed on me heavily, the not knowing. It was about a week later that I would go upstairs to see if the kids belongings had been moved about or into a different position.

As I got to the top of the stairs I saw scratches in the middle of one of the bedroom floors. I knew then it had to of been one of the spirits that had made those marks in the middle of the floor. As I walked into the room something pulled me towards the television set. As I walked up to it I decided to see of it still worked. So I reached out and attempted to turn it on.

As soon as I turned it on. I walked over towards the game system for the first time in a few weeks. As I turned to flip the switch on. From my left side I suddenly saw a figure in all white moving just barely inside of my line of sight. I turned towards the figure and sure enough. There she was once more, the lady in an all white wedding dress yet again.

She seemed to move beside me so gracefully. But it also felt as if she were trying to guide me to a different place at that moment. My instincts kicked in again. I followed her towards the stairs as she slowly faded into thin air disappearing on me yet once again. I continued to head back down towards the 1st floor for safety.

(Chapter 26)

As I got back down to the bottom of the stairs I heard loud banging coming from the basement once again. As if something were upset for some reason. I wasn't sure if it were upset by the fact that I'd went back upstairs. Or if it were upset that the lady in the White wedding dress had showed up once again. It was all starting to slowly come together now.

I was starting to figure out just what was going on. The ghost lady was their to keep me safe. As if she were a protector, a form of guardian angel. The evil spirits were there to remove me from the house. I didn't know if the man who had been killed there was the evil spirit. Or if the spirits had came there to take his soul upon his death.

There was definetly a fight between good and evil going on in our home. And my family had stepped right in the middle of it all. That's what it seemed to be to me at that time. The evil spirits weren't affected as bad as I thought they'd be by the Holy water being brought into and spread all about the house. It had only made a difference for a few days at the most.

Now it seemed to be that the spirits had came back even stronger than ever before. The sounds coming from all if the rooms were even louder than before. Things sounded as if they were being thrown about the place. I had stopped feeding the fire place the necessary wood in order to keep the house warm. The electric was turned off now.

The house was so cold you could see your breath now. I had plenty of blankets to stay warm and cozy. But you could see your breath inside of the house now. I had to get fire wood and soon. Or I would freeze if it got any colder inside. So I quickly ran over to the woods. I had wood already stacked over there. I just had to get it from point A to point B and fast.

(Chapter 27)

Once I got to the fence outside I quickly looked back over towards the house. I felt as if I had eyes on me now. That was a wild ass feeling to have. In the dark and residing at a haunted house. Where I had multiple spirits living with me. Everyone thought I was insane for staying up on Maple Drive. Even the neighbors had said that themselves to my family.

Everyone that lived on the street said that the house was creepy as hell. And that they felt something had been off about that house from day one if being built. I got the wood back inside. But I wasn't making a move toward the basement until the day light hours. No Way In hell would I even attempt to load the fire place.

I ate dinner as I sat in the kitchen. With 40 candles spread about the room. Burning in several different locations for lighting. That way atleast I could see if anything was coming for me. Always fearing in the back of my head. That I would eventually see the Devil. Or some other form of evil demons breath coming my way.

It was definetly a messed up situation to have to go through. But it was that or lose to evil. And I just didn't want to give up and lose our home. But I didn't think that I would be able to out stay the evil that was lurking about. It definitely felt like a powerful demon or spirit that had taken over. And was trying to force me out by imposing fear upon me at every moment available.

And for the most part it had been on point. When coming to unleashing it's power over the house itself. The throwing of materialistic possessions around the rooms of the house. The moving of objects into different locations as well showing me its power to manipulate things. I was really focused at this point to not give up. But it had come to be to me that the situation was just about hopeless.

(Chapter 28)

I made it until morning once again. Even though I awoke to be about half frozen. I had to get to the fire place fast. It had become so much colder during the night hours. Snow had fallen once again. Several inches had moved in over the night time. I got up and made my move towards the basement. I tried to set aside my fear. So I could get down there to get a fire going.

Nothing made itself present in that moment. So I kept pushing on forward. As I carried an arm full of fire wood. I threw the stack into the fire pit. And sprayed some lighter fluid on the wood itself. Then grabbing a wad of paper from a nearby notebook. I ripped it and wadded it all up into several balls and threw them into the fire place. Then lighting my lighter the flames kicked up.

I knew then that it would only be minutes until I would be warm once again finally after a few days of freezing. Living off of cold pop and canned goods at the time. It had been all about survival. To not give up to the will of the evil that lurked about. It would take a lot to push me out of our house. The fear had subsided for the most part. Giving me a break if only for a moment from the torment.

I was totally in it to win it now. To over come this damn evil shit that had been spreading fear around my family for weeks on end now. Nobody would even come up and check on me now. Hell I had to walk down the hill to grab supplies in order to make it. It was crazy that Noone would attempt to help anymore. They had all clearly given up on living at the house anymore.

I would be able to get a ride back up sometimes. But only to the top of the hill. Noone wanted to even drive on the street anymore out of fear. Which struck me as odd. I now started to wonder if my brother and his girlfriend new more than what they were telling me. Something was off about the two of them. And I could feel it just by looking at the both of them.

(Chapter 29)

They had without a doubt found out more than I'd known that was for sure. I could see the look in their eyes as they dropped me off each and every time after my visits to see mom and dad down below on the halfway point of the hill. I knew then that no one was ever coming back home ever again. And that was for sure certain.

The decision had already been made and was locked in for sure. So if I were going to decide to keep the house I'd be on my own from here on out. And that was a huge release of pressure on my shoulders. I was so happy it had finally been lifted from off of me. Finally after weeks of hell I had gone through on my own. Being left to defend the home front all by myself.

It wouldn't be to long after that I would also give up my fight on keeping the house from the grasps of evil. It wouldn't be that easy to give up and walk away for me either. As I knew I had given it my all without a doubt. I'd given it 100 percent of my soul to try and keep the house in our possession. From the evil spirits that had taken full control.

So if they were giving up, to hell with it I was also giving up as well. Why risk my life for nothing, that was my outlook on the whole damn situation. It would be a few nights later that all hell would break loose again. The weather would take a drastic turn and for certain would change the whole situation yet once again.

It would warm up a little bit the next few days as a warm front would move into our city. It also had brought heavy rains with it as well. The rain poured for two days straight. And on both of those nights the activity was so high. And had now moved all through the house also. In every room there was something going on. The basement had also became flooded during the rain storm.

The lights were turning off and on as I knew that weren't possible. As the power had been off for weeks now. The hallway chime clock was also going off and had been broken for years before we'd moved in. That's when I decided to pack up and leave for good. The spirits were at an all time high in power at the moment. There was no way in hell that I could win the fight at this point of the battle.

I wasn't risking my safety any longer. It just wasn't worth it to me anymore. I felt alone in the fight as of late. As I blew out all of the candles the house felt so cold all of a sudden. The fight was over and I walked out the back door. Locking up the door jam itself to keep others out as well as safe also from this evil ass place. I would then walk around to the front. Making sure it was also locked. To ensure the protection of others.

As I walked to the front of the driveway I could feel eyes on me from the top side window of the house. The feeling overwhelmed me as I got goose bumps allover my body. Not one family member ever went back there again after that day. So many family possessions had been left behind out of fear. From video games and televisions. To expensive clothes and washers and dryers also.

(Chapter 30)

(Reflection)

Looking back on the lives of my siblings as well as myself. I'd have say that we lived in several haunted locations as we'd all grown up in many locations and across several parts of town also. Sony strange experiences we had all been put through as we grew up together. Living in places where others had taken their lives or just passed from old age or natural deaths.

It seemed to me from all of the incidents that had occurred amongst my family and I. That I had come to the conclusion that these energies must had been drawn to my family. Nothing could be explained as to why we'd experienced so damn many hauntings over the years. It was all definetly a learning situation for me as I would experience so many other wild things on my own.

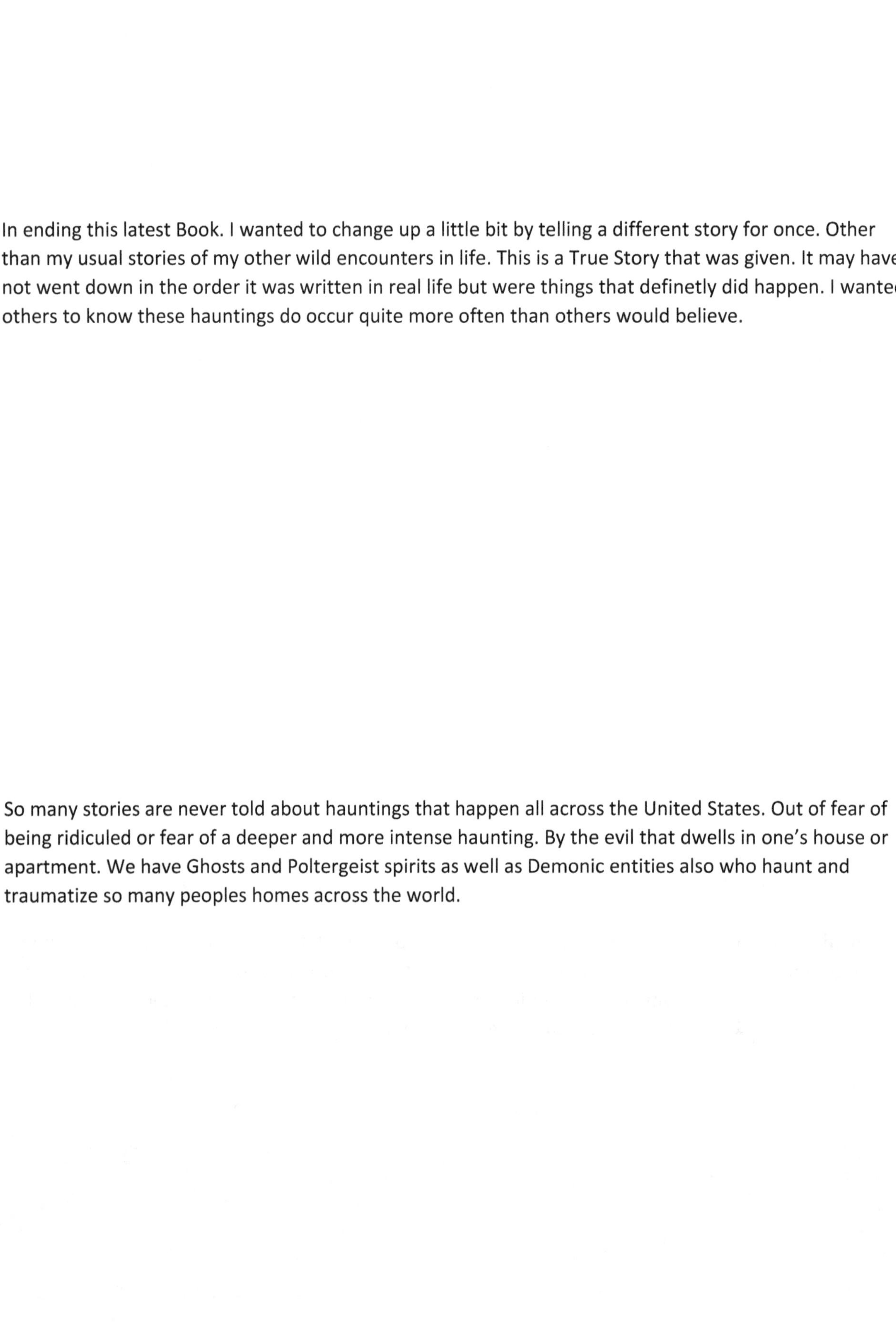

In ending this latest Book. I wanted to change up a little bit by telling a different story for once. Other than my usual stories of my other wild encounters in life. This is a True Story that was given. It may have not went down in the order it was written in real life but were things that definetly did happen. I wanted others to know these hauntings do occur quite more often than others would believe.

So many stories are never told about hauntings that happen all across the United States. Out of fear of being ridiculed or fear of a deeper and more intense haunting. By the evil that dwells in one's house or apartment. We have Ghosts and Poltergeist spirits as well as Demonic entities also who haunt and traumatize so many peoples homes across the world.

There are things one can do in order to try and save your home front. Holy water being one option. Or one could have a priest come and bless the home as well. Over my years of hauntings we have used many options as we possibly could to save our family from hauntings. Some worked and some options didn't work at all. You have to be careful how you tread water when you finally come to terms that your property has spirits dwelling among you.

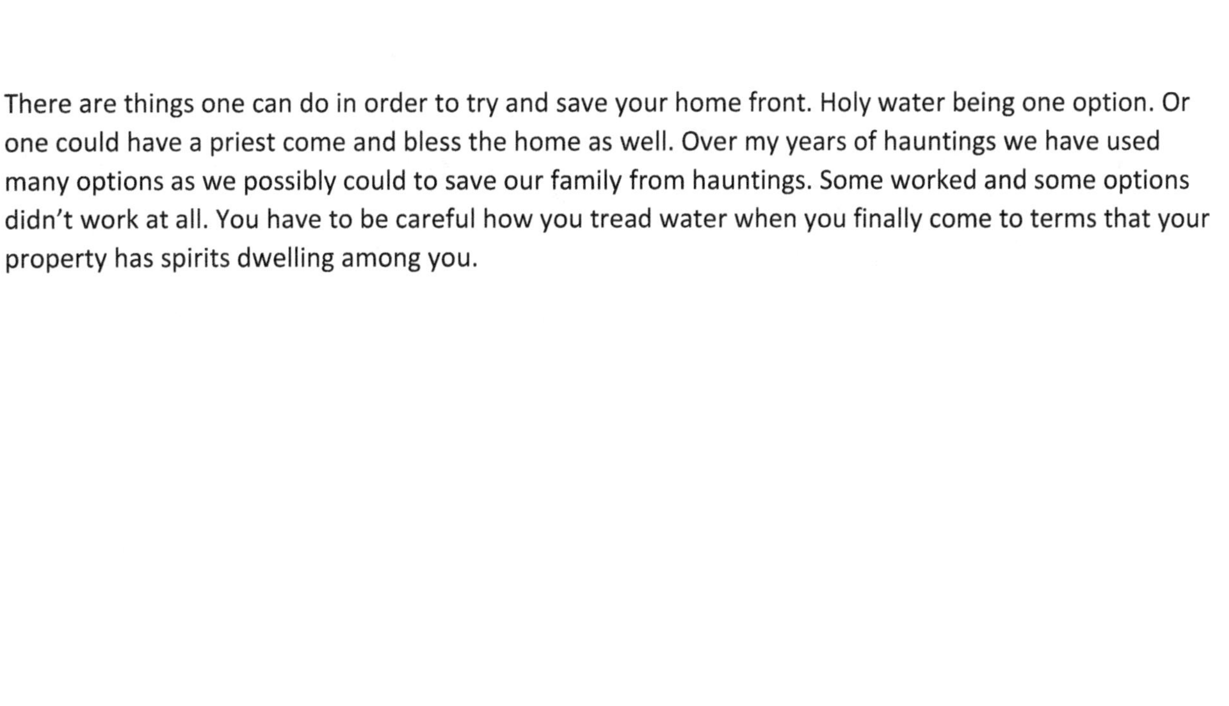

(Written By Jeffrey Lilly)

(July 29th 2022)

This book is dedicated to my family. As we were all put through constant hell and torment by evil spirits during this process in our lives. From house to house and or apartment we would move as we grew up. Only to experience some sort of spiritual. From the smallest of hauntings to the most traumatic and almost poltergeist types as well.

(The End)